CLOSE ENOUGH

A KATE FOX NOVELLA

SHANNON BAKER

SEVERN RIVER
PUBLISHING

CLOSE ENOUGH

Severn River Publishing
www.SevernRiverBooks.com

ISBN: 978-1-64875-059-5 (Paperback)

ALSO BY SHANNON BAKER

The Kate Fox Mysteries

Stripped Bare

Dark Signal

Bitter Rain

Easy Mark

Broken Ties

Exit Wounds

Double Back

Michaela Sanchez Southwest Crime Thrillers

Echoes in the Sand

The Desert's Share

The Nora Abbott Mystery Series

Height of Deception

Skies of Fire

Canyon of Lies

Standalone Thrillers

The Desert Behind Me

To find out more about Shannon Baker and her books, visit

severnriverbooks.com/authors/shannon-baker

CLOSE ENOUGH

I had no good reason to be out and about, except in my experience, sitting around on a bad day only made things worse. The cold night air scoured my cheeks and pinched my nose. Icy fingers seeped through my jeans to burn my thighs. My hands tingled in my pockets, but I'd had the good sense to pull a knitted cap over my ears. The forecast—something any decent Sandhiller kept track of, even if they didn't have cows to worry about anymore—predicted snow by midmorning tomorrow.

I could have stayed at home, snuggled under a blanket, propped on pillows, my nose in a paperback. But I couldn't focus on the words. TV held no interest for me, and my feet wouldn't stay still.

Every so often Mom made some rustling or banging sound in the basement. She'd started a new sculpture and couldn't be disturbed by me needing distraction. Dad was working, halfway on his way to Lincoln as conductor on the BNSF Railroad.

Any brothers or sisters around the county were at the wedding. They didn't want to be there, of course. But this was Grand County, population 1500. Absence of the whole Fox clan would cause gossip, probably cast me in a bad light as a bitter ex, and not help my election chances. Besides, an event this public provided a great opportunity for my family to quietly, or not so quietly, campaign on my behalf.

I drew the line on my attendance, though. Even with the election only two weeks away, when I'd be better served to dress up, paste on my most accepting smile, and maybe even lift a glass in congratulations, I only had enough grace to not take a shotgun to the wedding party.

I stomped down the road along the railroad, my eyes traveling across the tracks and up to the top of Main Street. The Legion Hall's windows radiated light. Cars and pickups parked in every slot and ribbons festooned the four streetlights. Guess no one told Roxy that an all-out celebration with the church and dress and attendants, and, lord help me, a three-tiered wedding cake, was considered gauche for a second wedding. But then, what did Roxy know about gauche--the concept or the term?

That's just the kind of thinking I needed to avoid. Resentment wouldn't restore the rug that had been jerked out from underneath my life.

I wanted to be the triumphant ex, who weathered betrayal, losing my home, my livelihood, my hopes and dreams, by beating my ex-husband in an election for sheriff.

See? No bitterness.

The smell of greasy goodness wafting into the cold air and the lights spilling from the windows of the Long Branch invited me, like coming home from a long trail. A breeze picked up, and I inched my way down the slope to the railroad right of way, my focus now on the Long Branch sign.

The collection of SUVs and cars parked along the highway outside of the bar and grill surprised me until I remembered that duck and quail season had opened. In another three weeks, one week postelection, deer season would begin. Then Hodgekiss would fill up for real.

I humped up the other side of the tracks, trotted across the highway, and pushed into the Long Branch. A glass door opened into a vestibule about twice the size of an old-fashioned telephone booth. A body could go through a second glass door to the right, into the restaurant, or push though the left door into the bar. The menu and service didn't vary from one side to the other, but the restaurant had brighter lights, where the bar usually had more interesting activity.

Warm air, heavy with deep fry grease, stale beer, and undertones of bacon, wrapped around me with familiarity. I scanned the crowd, not seeing many locals, and hurried to my favorite bar stool. Halfway there, a gangly boy with more braces than teeth, slammed into me. His buddy, an equally awkward preteen in a worn Husker starter jacket, cracked up and ran off.

Before the tackler could apologize, a grizzled codger, maybe his grandfather, shouted. "Damn it, Tyler! You want to come on a hunting trip with me, straighten up and fly right."

Gramps immediately turned his attention back to the group gathered around three tables shoved together. He raised a glass of what looked like whiskey, and joined their roar of drunken laughter.

Tyler mumbled an apology and slunk off to find his not-so-loyal Husker friend.

Ignoring the over-lubricated hunters and keeping an eye out for any more flying bodies, I hoisted myself on my seat. A kid, probably around ten years old, sat a couple of stools down, head bent over his phone. Soft hair, the color of a baby deer, hid his face.

Aunt Twyla drew beer from the Coors Lite tap and plunked the glass on a cork-lined tray. She slid the tray toward Bridgett Osentowski, who must have dropped out of her first semester of college and come home. "Take the beers to them guys by the pool table. Tell 'em they're on me on account of it taking so long to get their sandwiches."

Without waiting for Bridgett to react, Twyla swung toward the back room, scurrying her scrawny frame, her surprisingly thick hair swinging in the ponytail down her back, and started yelling. "I swear, Bud, if you don't get your butt in gear, I'm gonna give away more than we make..." There was more, but it grew increasingly profane as she disappeared into the kitchen.

Bridgett looked harried and scared. I had reservations about her lasting long working for Bud and Twyla. She glanced at me, then the tray, torn between taking my order and doing Twyla's bidding.

I nodded at the tray. "Take that. I'll wait."

Twyla rushed from the kitchen, a towel tucked in the back of her jeans, an unlit cigarette hanging from the corner of her mouth, and two thick plates full of burgers and fries. She stomped around the bar and slammed the plates on a table in front of two middle-aged men wearing crisp Carhartt overalls and clean hiking boots, with spanking new camo parkas hanging on the backs of their chairs.

As soft and pudgy as they looked, I didn't think they showed much wisdom in scowling at Twyla as if they expected cheerful service. They got off lucky when all she did was spin around, grab ketchup from a table where the hunters looked halfway done with their meal, and slapped it down between them. "Bon app-e-*tite*."

Twyla shot behind the bar. She pulled a rocks glass off the shelf by the cash register. Forget about two fingers, she splashed a whole hand of Jack Daniel's and lifted it to her lips. Her eyes shifted to me. Her eyebrows lifted, not making much impact on the wrinkles of her hard-living face, and she lowered the glass. "What?"

"You look busy."

She guffawed and ran a hand over her forehead, pushing back some of those inappropriately young-looking curls. She flicked her chin across the bar toward Bridgett. "She's not gonna work out."

I slid off the stool and slipped around the bar to rummage in the cooler. A hoppy microbrew caught my eye and I pulled it out. "Hello, beautiful."

Twyla took another gulp of bourbon. "Maybe you'll lose the election, and then you could work here."

I lifted my bottle to her. "That's a happy thought."

She caught Bridgett's eye and pointed her to a table of hunters. "Oh, I didn't mean it." She focused on me. "So, the Jackass and the Bimbo tied the knot. The whole town's at the Legion for the reception—damn lucky or we'd never be able to handle it." She gulped the bourbon. "You feel like killin' something?"

The beer felt like a glob of Play-Doh in my gut. "I'm fine."

Twyla studied me. "Yeah. Fine as a duck drowning in a cow pie."

I shrugged. Whining, crying, or throwing myself in a raging river wouldn't change the fact that Ted, my ex-husband for the last four months, husband for the eight years prior to that, had an affair with his high school sweetheart. Even though he'd balked at our divorce and pleaded with me not to go through with it, his heartbreak had lasted just long enough for the spring calves to be turned out to summer pasture. And now, two weeks after weaning those calves, he and Roxy, and everyone I'd known all my life, were dancing and drinking and celebrating their new lives together.

The Long Branch, the only watering hole in a thirty-mile radius, brought in families for a quick burger, dates for steaks and wine (great beef, not particularly good wine), ranch hands in for a cold one, and anyone and everyone else in Hodgekiss or just passing through. Most times, empty tables outnumbered full, but Saturday nights usually brought out a crowd.

I didn't mind the noisy bar filled with strangers. No one here knew I'd been kicked off the ranch I'd loved and now lived upstairs in my parents' house. They weren't spying on me when I wasn't looking, trying to figure out how I was holding up. No drunk cowboy tried to convince me the cure for my broken heart was naked rodeo with him.

I settled onto my stool and sipped the bitter beer, letting the jovial voices of the hunters rise and fall around me. Twyla hightailed it to the kitchen, berating Uncle Bud about the orders backing up.

Twyla returned with a plate and placed it in front of the kid. He set his phone down, smiled up at her and said thank you. That earned him a smile in response. Twyla picked up her glass and walked to me, twirling the amber liquid. "That danged Dahlia had the nerve to come in here the other day, passin' out Vote for Ted buttons."

I choked on the beer. That was audacious, even for Dahlia. "And she's still standing?"

Twyla's voice sounded like a shovelful of sand. "She ain't stupid. She come in here like she was having rolls and coffee with the other Flower Sisters."

Dahlia, my not-so-loving ex-mother-in-law, wore the queen's crown and ruled her sisters, Rose and Violet.

"She waited until Bud left for his morning break and I was back in the kitchen, then she struck. Like a fox, that one is." Twyla picked up her unlit cigarette and stuffed in back in the corner of her mouth.

She cackled. "I come around the corner with a trayful of clean coffee cups and there she is, bold as paint, tellin' Aileen and Jack Carson what a stand-up guy her scum-bucket son is. I pitched one of them cups like Eric Crouch when the Huskers won the national championship."

I shouldn't have laughed. But I'm no saint.

"I missed, and broke a perfectly good mug, but it was worth it to see her skedaddle out of the place."

I started in with the same lecture I'd given to my friends and all my brothers and sisters. "Don't hate the Conners on my behalf. The sooner—"

Twyla waved her hand. "Yeah, yeah. I ain't holdin' no grudge. Dahlia and Sid, hell, even Ted and Roxy can come in here for a beer and burger any time they want. But I draw the line on campaigning for that louse."

She threw her arm out and highlighted the red, white, and blue bedecked poster attached to the cash register at the end of the bar. "I got my own candidate and she's a humdinger." She high-fived me. "Even if I'd druther she be bartending for me."

I sipped my beer. "Yeah, that's not going to happen."

Most of the hunters merged together in an indistinguishable muddle. Camo, days' old beards, hair spiked and greasy from wearing hats and caps all day. The whole bunch had a tipsy, vacation vibe like a men's soccer team after a victory. For a lot of them, I suspect the men's time away from work and home, a soldiery brothers-in-arms, was the draw of hunting as much as the guns and stalking.

A group of four or five teens, the two involved in my hit-and-run included, slipped in and out of the side door. Maybe they procured their own bottle or a pack of smokes. The kid next to me seemed content with his burger and phone for company.

Twyla spun away without warning, hollering to Uncle Bud, and shot into the kitchen.

The door opened and I glanced up at the mirror above the bar. It was as if someone struck a match to kindling of feel-good inside me, and I grinned. Not so alone after all.

Sarah, my best friend and the woman married to my favorite brother, wound her way around the hunters, giving a couple of them sour looks. Her scowls didn't seem to bother them, though, as more than a few of them let their eyes trail her across the room. A red dress clung to her curves, and thick brown hair swathed her back. I wasn't beautiful and mysterious like Sarah. When we were young and single—I mean single the first time—Sarah always drew guys to our circle.

Bridgett stood paralyzed behind the bar, maybe terrified of Twyla swooping in again.

Sarah hoisted herself to the stool next to mine and addressed Bridgett. "Two Jacks on the rocks."

I grinned at her. "You're supposed to be eating wedding cake and toasting the bride and groom."

Sarah accepted the shots Bridgett slid in front of us and lifted hers. "We stayed long enough to be neighborly. But when Roxy brought out her guitar to sing 'God Bless the Broken Road,' I thought leaving would be nicer than puking on the bride."

"Understood." I picked up my glass and we tapped them together, then downed the acid, letting it burn away thoughts of the wedding.

Sarah nodded to Bridgett and held up two fingers, but Bridgett scuttled from the bar, probably sensing Twyla's return. Guess Sarah was determined to get me drunk. It also meant something else. "You're not pregnant."

She looked away from me and stiffened her neck. "Nope." In the way of us, that was all that needed to be said. She didn't have to tell me of her disappointment. I knew, just as she knew how wrecked I felt, try as I might to hide it.

"So." She turned back to me. "I talked to lots of people tonight and I think you've got the votes all sewed up."

The election loomed like the grim reaper, ready to slice off my head. I would probably lose. "Who would vote for me against Ted? He's been sheriff for two terms and did a fine job."

Sarah hmphed. "Unless you count last April." When he'd been shot, a local rancher had been murdered, and I'd solved it all to keep Ted from jail.

"There were plenty at the wedding disgusted that Ted and Roxy treated you poorly and were getting married so quick."

"Some folks might take offense to Ted having an affair with Roxy and betraying me, but enough to throw their vote my way?" I shook my head in doubt.

If I didn't get elected, it left me with a sticky problem of finding a job. I could keep living with Mom and Dad; they had the room for me since they'd raised nine kids in their house. All of them were grown and on their own. Except me, of course.

Since April, I'd earned enough from day labor to make my slight ends meet and pay rent to Mom and Dad. Fencing, cattle work, haying, wherever and whenever an extra hand was needed. Not satisfying and not particularly well-paying if you count the lack of anything resembling benefits.

Sarah tried to get Bridgett's attention and failed. "You're going to win, no doubt, but are you sure that's what you want?"

"Why not? Ted might have been the one driving around, throwing candy at parades, issuing traffic tickets, but you and I know that if it came to real detective work, it was me who did it."

She agreed readily. "But there is all that other stuff he did. Like paperwork or reports and going to meetings, and being diplomatic and who knows what all."

Bridgett hurried from table to table, serving drinks, getting orders. The Jack I'd downed, along with the beer, was doing me fine. But Sarah seemed determined for shot number two.

I played with my empty glass. "If Ted could do it, it can't be too tough."

She agreed and when the door opened, we both glanced at

the mirror. My brother Robert gave me a salute. Sarah pushed herself from the stool. "Sorry about not getting another shot. But you should probably go home now, anyway. Think of a campaign strategy to beat that pencil-dick. And come out tomorrow to help us move cattle closer to home. It's supposed to snow."

I knew I should follow Sarah's advice and head home. Let Ted and Roxy launch into their new life and wish them well. I wished them lots of things—chicken pox in August, electricity outages in January, years of discontent—but *well* would take some time and effort on my part.

Two stools down the bar, working on one of Bud's triple-decker burgers and a haystack of fries, the kid sat with his head propped on his hand. He looked bored or tired, maybe both. His father probably brought him on this male bonding trip, and left the kid to his own devices while he yukked it up with his cronies.

The kid double-fisted the burger and chomped it, eyes wandering over to me. I greeted him and waited for him to swallow. "How's the hunting?"

A slice of brown hair slipped down his forehead and he tossed his head to swish it out of big brown eyes. Windburned pink brushed his soft cheeks. "Our group bagged a bunch of geese and ducks. They got some quail, too."

"What about you?"

He glanced behind him again. "I don't like hunting."

I nodded. "Me, either."

He accepted that. "But you're a girl. You're not supposed to."

Not sure I could change his attitude in one casual conversation, I didn't bristle. "I'd rather hike or ride my horse, or do something else outside than sit in a blind and wait for birds."

He smiled that kind of kid smile that made me want to ruffle his hair and hug him. "You ride horses? Man, I'd love to do that."

If I still lived at Frog Creek and had access to horses, I'd invite the kid out tomorrow instead of him having to go hunting with a bunch of hungover urban warriors.

He munched a french fry. "I thought I'd like it. I mean, I'm in Boy Scouts and we camped and learned all this cool stuff about setting up camps and outdoor survival. But hunting is a lot of sitting around."

"Hey, Ethan." A slight man with light-colored hair and a thin scruff of blond beard threw an arm around the kid. "Who's your lady?"

Ethan colored and stared at his plate. This must be the man responsible for giving Ethan the idea that girls shouldn't hunt. If it weren't for Ethan, I'd have ignored him. But I wanted to take the attention away from the poor kid, who didn't deserve to be embarrassed for talking to me.

I held my hand out. "I'm Kate."

The guy slapped his palm on the back of Ethan's head. "Ethan is a real ladies' man." He took my hand. "I'm Tony. Brought my nephew out here on his first hunting trip. It's the rite of passage for our clan. My dad brought me and my brother out here when we were Ethan's age. So I'm doing the uncle thing and making sure the kid gets to do it, too. My sister isn't married so I'm the man in Ethan's life."

Isn't that nice. Every kid needs a jerk to look up to. I mentally slapped myself for my rush to judgment. Tonight, any man over Ethan's age wasn't likely to get a fair shake with me. "I'm sure you'll have a great time."

Even though I shifted forward and hunched over my beer a little, the guy didn't take the hint. He stepped up to the bar stool between me and Ethan and rested one hip on it. "I'm from Omaha. I'm a CPA."

CPA Tony from Omaha didn't need to carry his Smarmy Card for me to know he wasn't my type. I tossed him a discouraging one-quarter smile and studied my beer.

He persisted. "So, you're from around here? What do you guys do for fun? When it isn't hunting season, I mean."

I glanced at the mirror over the bar. Ethan had devoured half his hamburger and made a dent in the fries. He looked up and caught my eye, and I swear those big brown eyes sent me a sincere apology for his uncle's boorishness. I think Ethan and I could be friends. I winked at him and he grinned back.

Tony leaned on the bar, blocking my view of Ethan. "My aunt lives here. You might know her—Deb Holt?"

I could tell Tony that Deb's dog, an Australian shepherd blue heeler mix, was named Buster and Deb baked the worst lemon meringue pie in the county. She made garish Christmas wreaths, one of which graced my front door at Frog Creek since she'd given it to us for a wedding gift. She and Dahlia were so tight they had to unzip if one went on vacation.

He gave me a loose smile. "She usually cooks a big meal for us on Saturday night of opening season, but she had a big wedding or something."

Yeah, or something.

"So, we're here. It's fortunate, or I'd never have met you."

And our relationship felt so meaningful.

"I thought everyone out here was related or something. How come you're not at the wedding?"

I drank my beer and didn't answer. Tony didn't seem to notice.

All the while, Tony leaned closer, his whiskey breath washing over me. "So, Ethan and I have a room upstairs. But Ethan, he likes to play games on his phone, so he's good down here for an hour or so."

"This is your bonding time with your nephew. I couldn't

interfere with that." I should have left it at that, but this wasn't a great night for me and men. "Besides, you're a creep."

I didn't know Twyla had been watching the whole scene, but her cackle made Tony whip his head up and frown. Without another word to me, Tony motioned to Ethan. "You about done?" He stomped off to his group. Ethan gifted me with another cute grin, then slipped off his stool, leaving his decimated meal behind him as he followed his uncle.

I wound the scarf around my neck, pulled on my cap, buttoned up, and hit the door into the frigid night. I should go home. Barring that, I'd be better served to walk out of town and wander a dark country road until I wore myself out.

I turned up Main Street. Did I want to torture myself? Vehicles not only lined the street heading up to the Legion, but side streets also looked like parking lots. I counted my sister, Louise's old Suburban, brother Michael's shiny Ford pickup, Douglas's university-issued Jeep Wagoneer, Jeremy's dented Ford. With Sarah and Robert on their way home, that accounted for all my brothers and sisters in the county. I knew they only attended to help me out, so why did I feel betrayed?

See? I was right. I shouldn't have come up here. I turned to hurry down the hill, but before I got to the Long Branch, the sound of boys laughing, someone barfing, and the smell of cigar smoke wafted from the alley next to the bar.

Despite mind-blowing technological advances, some things, particularly in Hodgekiss, never changed. The only difference for me is that now, I was the disapproving adult, not the recalcitrant kid. I paused at the mouth of the alley and folded my arms.

The Husker kid noticed me first, and he took off on a dead run out the other end of the alley. One kid stayed on his hands and knees, head hung toward a puddle of vomit. Four other boys stood around him in various stages of alarm.

I deepened my voice to sound stern. "You boys get back inside." I extended my arm. "Hand over the booze and cigars."

The tallest kid tossed his head. "We don't have—."

The kid who'd run into me earlier shoved the tall one. "Forget it. Give it to her."

Glad they didn't put up a fight, I accepted their nearly empty bottle of Wild Turkey and their last cigar. The kid on the ground staggered to his feet and the boys filed out of the alley. I hated to see Ethan, the smallest and youngest by a few years, in tow with the older boys. Head down, he lifted his eyes for a shamed second and slumped off.

I'd had enough of the evening and beat cleats to my parents' house to watch movies on TMC until the wee hours.

——————

My phone woke me a few hours after dawn. I'd never slept this late when I lived at Frog Creek. There. That's a good thing about not being a rancher anymore. The phone rang again, and I thought hard before snaking my hand from the cocoon of quilts. Milky autumn sun struggled through the open curtains, not bright enough to afford any warmth to my childhood bedroom on the second story of my parents' house.

I snagged the phone and burrowed deeper into my bed. Sarah sounded breathless, and the static rumble of a pickup on the road rattled her voice. "What have you heard?"

This wasn't good. I stretched my feet to the freezing sheets at the bottom of my bed, wide awake. "About what?"

Her voice pulled away from the phone, talking to Robert, I assumed. "She doesn't know anything." To me: "A kid's gone missing. One of the hunters. News came over the police scanner at Mom's, and she called. We're heading in to help the search."

I whipped the quilt back and jumped up. "What kid? Where is everyone gathering?"

"You know what I know, except we're meeting at the Long Branch. I hope you get elected because I like having the inside scoop."

My feet, nearly numb from the icy floor, hopped to the top of the stairs and propelled me down to the relative warmth. "I'll meet you there."

I hoped Dad was home from his last trip and had made coffee. More importantly, he had a preternatural ability to know everything in the county. He could fill me in on the details of the missing kid.

Sadly, no coffee in the pot, only the rattling of Mom in the basement, still in her creative mania.

In less than twenty minutes, I'd showered, dressed in my warmest, from long johns to insulated coveralls, and joined a gathering crowd at the Long Branch, sipping Twyla's chest-hair-growing java and trying to get information. Along with neighbors and friends, all the daily faces of my life, hunters in their camo and Cabela's chic gathered with worried faces.

All those boys in the alley last night, it could be any one of them, but I pictured Ethan. His expressive dark eyes and silky hair falling across his forehead. I'd wanted to hug him and protect him last night. That urge only grew the longer we waited for information.

I found Michael, Douglas, Robert, and Sarah at the corner of the bar. They were similarly outfitted as I was, all ready to face the frosty morning searching for a lost kid.

The bar was packed, the noise level high, electric worry passed from one knot of folks to another. Along the bar, Violet and Rose, Ted's aunts, seemed out of place. They weren't known for their outdoorsy ways, and neither wore heavy weather gear. Violet's back faced me, her short hair permed and teased. Rose's eyes glittered with excitement, as if watching a football game or action movie. Violet's arm tugged at something and twisted, and my campaign poster slipped from its place on the cash register and fell to the floor, where Violet wiped her boots on it.

Rose laughed, then her eyes lit on me and she froze, turned red, and backed into the crowd.

The door opened and everyone stirred. Voices escalated, feet shuffled, and people moved aside to let the entourage into the middle of the bar.

Dang it. Even though I'd braced for it, had my fences shored up and gates closed, the first glance of Ted shattered me. He leaned on his cane, still unsteady from the gunshot he'd taken to his spine in April. Despite that, he had the powerful look of confidence. Dark hair, a scruff of whiskers that would be thick come evening, broad shoulders, and all that dreamy attractiveness I'd gotten used to in our eight years of marriage. I began my mental litany to gain perspective: *He cheated. He lied. He betrayed me. What I thought was love was my imagination. I'm better off without him.*

All of that happened in a heartbeat, and I inhaled a stabilizing breath, fairly certain if anyone had been watching me, they'd never see the battle under the surface.

Roxy flounced beside Ted, one hand protectively on his shoulder, the other out, like an offensive lineman protecting the halfback. Instead of shoulder pads and helmet, she shone with her usual flash and sparkle, wearing a low-cut, rhinestone-studded T-shirt and puffy down vest. She chirped like a self-important canary—a newly married one. "Careful. You don't want to reinjure the sheriff. Give him some space so everyone can hear him."

Conversation dwindled and the room quieted. Ted took to his spotlight like a cat in a basket of warm laundry. He didn't smile, of course, that wouldn't look good. But he played the hero like Ben Affleck, down to the square chin. "Thank you, every-one, for coming out today. As you've heard, we've got a little boy missing. His name is Ethan Holt."

Even if I'd suspected, hearing his name was a punch to my heart.

Ted spread his concern to each person, making eye contact. "Ten years old. He's from Omaha. Last seen just before daybreak."

Another stir by the door and the crowd spit out Tony, with a tearful Deb Holt behind him. Tony's face flushed crimson, and he stuttered. "M-m-m-my nephew. We were hunting up on my aunt's alfalfa field. I don't know what happened. Ethan was there and we flushed the birds. When I turned around, he was gone."

Deb broke down in wails. "He's a city kid. And the snow's fixing to start."

Dahlia stood behind Deb. She patted Deb's back and her lips moved, probably in comforting words. But Dahlia's eyes scanned the room with calculation. No doubt she weighed how the popular vote played out for Ted.

Ted stood tall, putting his weight on his good leg, not using his cane. "Just beyond that alfalfa pivot is the Middle Loup River. Lots of rushes and cattails. There's any number of cattle or wildlife trails Ethan could have taken."

Deb spun around and threw her arms around Dahlia.

The longer Ted stood there, the more he looked like Super-man, all broad-chested and full of purpose. Dahlia's eyes gleamed with pride as she watched him. Pride and something else. Satisfaction?

Ted's gaze swept across the room. He pointed to the far corner. "Tuff, you take a bunch and start at the east end of the Holt headquarters."

Several people murmured their affiliation with Tuff's contingent. Ted continued to assign areas to different groups. The hunters, as well as the Sandhillers, seemed to gather strength from Ted's command.

Because I couldn't stand to look at Ted anymore, my gaze rested on Dahlia. I caught the sly look, lasting shorter than a sparrow's heartbeat, that passed between her and Tony.

My focus shifted to Tony. When he'd spoken to us, he'd been distraught. But now, with no one paying attention to him, he looked less than worried. He even managed a sleazy smile in my direction.

Sarah slapped my arm. "Let's go."

I must have given her a blank expression. She snapped her fingers in front of my face as if releasing me from a trance. "The south fork of the Loup? The Foxes are searching there."

My gaze tripped back to Tony, who didn't appear to be in a hurry to find Ethan. Dahlia left Deb's side and made her way to Ted and Roxy, her body language screaming victory.

I'd seen that look on Dahlia's face before. About a month before Ted and I were married, Dahlia had invited us to a competition at her shooting club in Broken Butte. Deep in the throes of new love, I'd have followed Ted down a raging water-fall. Back then, I hadn't learned Dahlia could be much more dangerous than any wild river. When Roxy just happened to be entered into the competition, I'd tried to give Dahlia the benefit of the doubt. But wearing the same smug expression on her face as today, she'd innocently reminded me how Ted and Roxy had been shooting champions in high school. Back when they'd been voted cutest couple at Hodgekiss High.

Sarah tugged on my arm. "Come on."

"No." The word slipped out without much thought.

Robert, Sarah's husband and my big brother by less than a year, whipped his head around. "No?"

His tone caught Douglas's and Michael's attention on their

way toward the door. The twins, looking as much alike as a cuddly teddy bear and a pit bull, spun to me. Michael, the dog, pulled his head back as if I'd slapped him. "There's a little boy out there, and you're not going to help find him?"

While plenty of people had already filed out, there were enough bunched at the door that I felt nailed with hostile eyes.

I didn't normally rejoice to see my oldest sister, Louise, but her voice punched through the blocked doorway, making me grateful for her distraction. "We'll set up headquarters here. Twyla will keep the coffeepot on and I've got snacks. Sandwiches at noon, of course."

She muscled her way against the tide, carrying a food service tray of cupcakes, several of them picked off by those leaving the Long Branch. Louise baked with the zeal of a half dozen Keebler elves on speed and was about the size and shape of double that many elves squished together. She set the tray on a table and stood back, waiting for praise.

When none of us said anything, she opened her hands toward the tray. "Genius, huh?"

I bent over the dozens of chocolate cupcakes. Vote for Kate Fox was piped in red onto each frosted top.

A self-congratulatory grin spread across her face. "I'm calling them Kate Cakes."

Michael grabbed a cupcake and shoved it in his mouth. Louise lunged for him, like Jell-O on skates. "Those are for the voters."

Michael's answer arrived muffled in cake. "Election's over. Kate lost."

Louise gasped. "Don't you say that. I know it doesn't look great right now, but there are still ten days before the election and if we all make an effort to get out there, Kate will—"

Douglas shook his head. "Ted set up the search and rescue, and Kate's refusing to go."

He had that wrong. "I'm not refusing. There's no need because Dahlia—"

Louise's eyes popped wide in shock, and her mouth started before she drew a breath. "You what? Of course you're going to look for him. Even if you didn't need to do it to show what a good citizen you are, you have to do it because he's a little boy in trouble."

Our little circle of Foxes all nodded in agreement, with most throwing in a "Yeah" or "That's right."

Almost everyone had filtered out of the Long Branch by then, leaving our clan to duke it out, me against everyone.

I knew Dahlia was up to something. At least, I thought I knew. "Dahlia staged this whole event." But what if I was wrong?

Louise rolled her eyes. Douglas's mouth quirked up, maybe in amusement. Everyone else carried various levels of disbelief. They all looked like a big pile of put-out.

Sarah spoke with her trademark frankness. "We know Dahlia likes to pull strings and watch the puppets dance. And if she could swing popularity in Ted's direction, she'd do that. But, really, using a kid? When there's a storm coming?"

Robert nodded. "That's low, even for Dahlia."

I had to defend myself now, even if that little sliver of doubt nagged at me. "Dahlia's manipulations have no bottom."

Louise planted her hands on her hips. "Are you trying to lose this election? After all we've done to help you get elected? I've been baking for six months straight. The kids put up posters everywhere."

Michael, alpha pit bull, joined in. "And I got you that speaking gig at the Lion's Club."

I didn't let that one go. "You invited Ted, too."

Michael shrugged. "I had to. But at least you got to say your piece."

Douglas, the teddy bear, slipped in an aside. "And you made more sense than Ted."

"But not enough to overcome him being a man." Robert licked frosting off his finger. "This election is close, even if there was no kid missing."

Sarah nodded. "I know I said you had it won, but I was only trying to give you confidence. Robert is right. You can't make a wrong move now or it's over."

Fighting them was futile, but I'm a sucker for a lost cause. "I'm telling you, there is no missing kid. Ethan's uncle isn't so upset he can't flirt with me, for heaven's sake. After everyone is worried and out there looking, Ted is miraculously going to find Ethan where no one else thought to look. He'll be the hero."

Their faces told me that if belief was an ocean, their faith in me wouldn't fill a thimble.

Michael spoke, the pit bull sinking his teeth in. "You're deluded, obviously. But let's say you're right. You still need to go through the motions or you look bitter."

Douglas never agreed with his twin, except now. "That's what you've been trying to avoid. Why we had to suffer through that awful wedding."

"I don't care if I win or lose." Which of course was a lie. "But I'm not playing Dahlia's game."

An eruption of arguments, cursing, guilt-tripping, and even some name-calling from childhood couldn't change my mind. With some dismissive flicks of hands, some raspberry blowing, and general annoyance of my unreasonable stubbornness that, according to them, had been my dominant personality trait since infancy, they slammed out the door to rescue a child who, no doubt, sat in comfort somewhere playing games on his phone.

I hoped.

I watched them leave, then turned to Twyla, who sipped a

steaming cup of coffee behind the bar. "Where is Louise? I thought she was going to help you with refreshments."

Twyla huddled around her mug, probably fighting her daily hangover. "My guess is she couldn't stand to be around someone so dug in they can't listen to reason."

I appealed to my last supporter. "You know Dahlia. This reeks of her conniving."

Twyla set her cup on the bar. "I saw that boy here last night. If there's any risk he's in trouble, I'd say you need to go find him."

"The only trouble he's in is being corrupted by Ted's mother."

Twyla swiveled on her heel and disappeared into the kitchen.

The Kate Cakes and I remained in the dim bar, watching the clouds sink lower over the icy morning, giving full warning of the snow heading our way. A whoosh of wind rattled the window, and I shivered. Ethan's puckish face taunted me. He didn't deserve to be used like this. I'd been offended when Tony had employed Ethan as a babe magnet, if you could even call me a babe, but this duplicity was worse.

In the wintery gloom outside the window, a pickup sped down the highway. Tricked out with lights along the interior dash and outlining the hood. Dahlia's royal coach, the rig that usually caused my gut to tighten with dread.

I grabbed my coat and ran out the door, determined to find out where she was going.

Following Dahlia might be tricky, since I'd driven my beloved '79 Ranchero, Elvis. I'd bought Elvis before I was old enough for a driver's license. I'd spent more than I could afford to repair his crushed back fender from the night Ted had been shot. It was the only thing I could fix about that night. Since my failed marriage, Elvis was the deepest and most lasting love in my life.

Dahlia headed east in gathering fog, and I took a guess she'd turn south on the highway, making her way to Frog Creek. Without the benefit of seeing her, I turned and set a slow pace for the five miles to the ranch turnoff. Ted and Roxy would have traveled the dirt road from the ranch that morning, but there could be extra tracks in the damp sand.

I *knew* Dahlia was finagling. Even if her smug face and crafty edge didn't give her away, my gut told me. But that didn't mean my tracking skills had brought me to the right place. And even if Dahlia was at Frog Creek, it didn't mean Ethan was here or that I'd get any confession from Dahlia Dearest.

What else did I have? Hanging around the Long Branch and getting hated on by family and foe? Going back to Mom and Dad's and pouting? Sure, I could join the search, go through the motions, and maybe salvage the election, but when Ted produced Ethan, safe and sound, he'd be the hero, and the votes would pile up in his favor.

Gritting my teeth, I pulled Elvis onto the lane and headed down the familiar road to my old home.

Elvis and I had traveled this road so many times I could probably let him take the wheel. Each hill tugged at my heart, the reds and golds, deep browns, and faded green of the fall grass popped in the damp gray of the morning. We didn't have lots of trees or the weather patterns that bring vibrant leaves, but autumn brought a special beauty to the prairie that seeped deep into me. I didn't want to, but I missed Frog Creek with a longing that clogged my throat.

I rounded the last hill heading down into the headquarters and the ranch house where Ted and Roxy now shared bliss. Chalk one up to my detecting skills, Dahlia's ostentatious pickup idled out front. I gunned Elvis down the lane and pulled him up, nose to nose. He had seen more miles, wasn't shiny and new, didn't have the horsepower, four-wheel drive, or heated seats, but Elvis had style and quality Dahlia's ride would never achieve.

So weird to walk up those wooden porch steps and stand in front of that door and not be able to reach out and turn the knob, walk in, and be home. I hesitated, unsure whether to knock or pound, or simply open the door and holler from the threshold. Instead of doing anything, I glanced through the window in the door and looked all the way through the living room and dining room to the warm glow of the kitchen. The ranch house had that shotgun shack layout. Dahlia passed by the opening in the kitchen holding a coffee cup. She laughed and said something.

I hadn't expected Roxy to be home. I figured she'd be side by side with Ted, where she'd stayed since he'd been shot at the Bar J, the night I discovered their affair.

Dang. That past was not relevant here. With a whoosh of cold air to fill my lungs, I landed the heel of my hand on the door twice and turned the knob. Holding back any emotion I did or didn't feel, I raised my voice to travel across the house. "Hello."

Dahlia jerked, sloshing coffee on her leg. She faced me with a horrified expression, mouth hanging open.

Roxy poked her head around the kitchen corner, surprise, confusion, and something like delight flashing all over her. "Kate? Oh my God, Kate!"

She flew from the kitchen and grabbed me by the arm, pulling me into the living room and shutting the door behind me. "What are you doing here? I mean, I'm so glad you came. I want you to always feel like our door is open to you. This was your home for a long time and just because—."

I tried to keep my mind riveted on Dahlia and let Roxy wax

on without really listening, but a part of me noticed that while most of the room looked the same as when I'd lived there, new artwork graced the walls, and couch pillows, a couple of end tables and new lamps made the whole place homier. That hurt.

Didn't Roxy ever breathe? "—tell Ted that I came home. He thinks I'm helping Louise but, honestly, I'm so tired from the wedding and reception that I thought I'd take a quick nap and be back before—."

Dahlia closed her mouth and hesitated only a second before heating up like a branding iron in the fire. She slammed the coffee cup on a counter hidden by the side of the entryway and strode toward me. "What in heaven's name are you doing here?"

Roxy's chatter dribbled off.

I steadied myself and faced Dahlia down. "Where is Ethan?"

Dahlia's disdainful laugh didn't convince me of her innocence. "What are you talking about? Ethan who?"

Roxy edged toward Dahlia. "It's okay. I don't mind Kate coming here. It's time we get to be friends. Ted always said we'd really like each other if we gave it a chance."

I stared at Dahlia. "There's a storm coming, and all those people out searching don't need to suffer through it. Let's call the game and get the kid back."

Dahlia flung her arm out with such force it was surprising it didn't fly out of her socket. "Deb's grandson is out there somewhere. Why aren't you searching for him?"

A light came on in Roxy's dim expression. "That's right. You should be helping the search."

If contempt were a dart, I'd have shot it through both their necks. "Are you in on it, too? Does Ted know what you're doing?"

Snap. Off went the bulb in Roxy's expression. "In on what?"

I advanced on Dahlia. "I'm going to say you planned this

fiasco yourself. I don't think Deb knows because she seemed sincerely upset."

Aside from teaching a kid how to lie and manipulate, Dahlia had unnecessarily traumatized one of her best friends. What a gal. "We've got freezing rain starting. That means treacherous roads and lots of good people out there. Get Ethan. I promise not to expose you or Ted."

Dahlia lifted her chin and gazed down her imperial nose at me. "You started this whole fight when you ran for office."

From my position, several inches shorter than Dahlia, I was tempted to send my fist crashing into her nose and splattering it across her face. Except I had no boxing skills and hadn't punched anyone since I'd grated my knuckles on my older sister's braces as a kid.

Dahlia wanted me to leave so she could get Ethan and take him where Ted was sure to find him. Ethan wasn't at the headquarters, or Roxy would know about it. A gust buffeted the white pine in the yard, and it clicked in my head, my heart slamming into my ribs. "You put him in the line shack on the old Mackleprang place, didn't you?"

Dahlia stuttered. "Mackleprang? What? Shack? You're crazy."

I lunged at her and grabbed her arm, shaking it. "You did, didn't you?" Another gust smacked into the side of the house, like an eighteen-wheeler on a bridge abutment.

Eyes wide, maybe afraid I would throw that punch I'd dreamed about, Dahlia stayed silent.

Roxy, apparently not as dim as I'd assumed, put it all together. "If Ethan's at the shack, it'll be okay. Ted and I were there a few days ago, and the heater works great. It's a little dusty but a kid won't mind that."

Dahlia still wasn't talking. And remembering how Ted and I used that shack on occasion, I didn't want to know what Ted and Roxy were doing there. I still had hold of Dahlia's arm and I squeezed. "Except the flue collapsed in a storm last year and I never got a chance to fix it. If you started the heater, a gust would send the fumes back down into the house. Ethan could suffocate."

"Oh." Her mouth worked in silence. Finally, Dahlia found her voice. "No." Not much, but enough.

I spun around and dashed for the door, across the porch, heading for Dahlia's four-wheel drive. Footsteps hit the wooden steps behind me, and before I got the pickup in gear, Roxy threw herself into the passenger seat.

Moisture-heavy clouds had shuffled into the valley while we'd been inside, and a combination of rain and ice gathered on the windshield. I cranked on the defrost and backed from Elvis, more than a little irritated to have Roxy riding shotgun. "What are you doing?"

She adjusted the temperature controls to allow maximum heat. "You might need help or something."

I swerved around rough patches in the road, knocking her into the door. "You don't even have a coat."

Roxy flung herself to her knees and rummaged behind the bucket seat of fine Corinthian leather. Triumphant, she whipped out a black down coat complete with fur-lined hood. "Dahlia always keeps a spare coat for emergencies."

Most Sandhillers' emergency gear consisted of used outwear one step away from the dump. Roxy pushed her arms into a brand-new down coat and zipped up, covering her masterpiece of a cleavage, a clear sign she took this seriously. "Besides, I needed to get away from Dahlia so I can process what she did."

Rocks pinged on the underside of the pickup as I sped down the gravel. Not sure what to think of the nugget Roxy dropped. I figured she and Dahlia thought with one mind, their hearts beating in rhythm to their adoration of Ted.

Across one Autogate, I made a quick right on a two-rut trail road.

Roxy clutched the "oh shit" bar above the door. "It would be faster if you go out to the oil strip and come in from that side."

As if Roxy knew Frog Creek better than I did. "Smoother doesn't mean faster. The cut-across is best." Dang. "Do you have your phone?"

She propped her other hand on the dash for support. "No." She turned to me. "Do you?"

"It's in Elvis."

Rain gave way to ice pellets that popped against the windshield. The sky dropped farther, dulling everything in a shroud of gray. The wind rocked against the pickup, a constant reminder that Ethan might be passed out or worse in a cabin filling with fumes.

I fought the wheel, keeping the tires in the ruts and giving it as much gas as I dared. "You and Ted had nothing to do with this?"

Her voice cracked, exaggerated emotion being her superpower. "You know Teddy loves kids. He'd have thought about the broken flue. He's so smart like that." She sniffed. "Like you."

"If you knew anything about your own place, you'd know about the flue." Disbelief charged through me so that I banged on the steering wheel. "What was Dahlia thinking pulling a stunt like this?"

Roxy umphed when I hit a bull hole in the road. "I love Dahlia, I really do."

There was a *but* following this, and I felt some vindication for all the years I'd had to put up with Dahlia's machinations.

Roxy sighed in admiration. "I know she did this out of love for Ted. I hope I have that kind of tiger love for my kids when we have them."

I'd let my hopes rise that underneath all that—Roxy, there was a decent human being. When would I learn?

I wrestled Dahlia's Flashmobile through the pasture, only stopping long enough to make Roxy dash to open gates.

Ice pellets gave way to sleet, sloppy and cold, smashing on the windshield and bringing the ever-welcome moisture to the hills. The clouds seeped low enough I might as well call it fog. It brought out the reds of the grass.

Even though it seemed like it took us as long as a moon circling Jupiter, we finally spotted the line shack across the hay meadow. The Sandhills used to be home to Indians, outlaws, and stray cattle lost on epic drives from Montana to Texas. Then a few brave or desperate souls tried their hands at home-steading. Though I didn't know much about the Mackleprangs, all of them long gone by the time Dad was a kid, their lost hopes and dreams nestled along the west edge of a tall hill. Cotton-woods and dying elms shaded a two-room house.

Ted's family had added a used stove and heater, secondhand furniture, and provided minimum maintenance to house a hired man or summer hay help if they needed it. From time to time they'd rented it out to deer hunters, but mostly, it remained empty.

I roared up to the house. The scruffy yard hadn't been mowed this year and looked only slightly more domesticated than the prairie surrounding it. Tracks ran along the dirt road to the east, with the oil strip just over the hill. The strip zagged its way to the highway.

Roxy and I jumped out and ran. She was closer to the house and made it to the front door first. She burst in, with me close behind. Both of us shouted, "Ethan!"

Our voices bounced back to us. It took two seconds to see Ethan wasn't in the house. Another two more to realize how toxic the air smelled.

I shouted at Roxy, "Open the window!"

The heating unit attached to the wall was the distinguishing mark between the kitchen and the sitting room. I dove for it and shut it off.

Roxy and I stood in the middle of the house, cold air working its way through the cramped space. "What now?"

I zipped my barn coat and pulled my cap from the pocket. "Find Ethan."

Roxy glanced at the fancy cowboy boots she'd worn to town, but didn't say anything. She pulled the hood up, shoved her hands into the pockets of Dahlia's coat, and marched out the door ahead of me.

The sleet kept driving down. Maybe the fog saved us a degree or two, but the temperature probably hovered around thirty. How long had Ethan been out in this? Did he wear his outdoor hunting gear? How long before a little guy with no meat on his bones succumbed to hypothermia?

Ethan's big brown eyes, that shock of silky hair, the cute grin. *Where are you?*

Even though Roxy was willing to brave the cold, I had insulated coveralls and hiking boots, more suited to time outside. "You take the pickup and drive to the top of the hill. Maybe you can see him from there."

She beelined for the truck. "See? That's what I mean. You're like Ted was this morning at the Long Branch. Thinking it through, making a plan."

Except Ted had sent gobs of people into the storm for no reason. There was only me and Roxy to find Ethan. I took off at a trot following the track road to the east, toward the oil strip. It seemed the easiest trail for a kid to take. I shouted into the fog, my voice falling to the prairie ground.

I strained to see anything moving. The constant yelling scraped my throat. I jogged a few steps. Stopped. Listened.

Started again. The gravel road behind me showed old tire tracks but no sign of my footprints. If Ethan came this way, he wouldn't have left evidence.

The rumble of the pickup was the only sound. Not even birds wanted to be out in this weather. The road formed a wide arc around the hill, and in about two miles, it connected with the oil strip.

What if Ethan hadn't taken the road? What if he'd wandered across the pasture? Taken one of dozens of cattle trails? The usual way to find him would be to get Chester McManus, Grand County old-timer, into his Cessna to fly the hills. But nobody was going up in this weather.

I ran harder, yelled louder. The image of Ethan curled up on the prairie, those wonderful eyes closed forever, that adorable smile never lifting his lips again, urged me on.

With no sign of Ethan, I came to the oil strip. The turnoff to the Mackleprang house sat in the dip between two hills to the north and south. I hesitated. Disoriented by fog, would Ethan turn south? Would he know north led the way to town?

Melted sleet soaked my coveralls. My socks, damp from sweat, chilled my feet. What kind of protection did Ethan wear?

From far away, the roar of Dahlia's pickup grew until Roxy pulled up next to me and slid the window down. The heat of the cab puffed across my cheeks. I needed to get Ethan out of this cold and into that comfort. "Anything?" I asked Roxy.

She shook her head and waited for instructions.

I nodded to the south. "Go that way. Honk your horn and call for him. I'll head north." The window slid up, but I slammed my gloved palm on it. "You don't need to go more than five miles. He couldn't have traveled any farther than that." I didn't watch her drive away.

A thin layer of slush accumulated on the one lane road but was not solid enough to hold a footprint. Why hadn't we brought phones? Someone might have come along the road and picked him up. He could be back at the Long Branch right now, enjoying hot chocolate and a Kate Cake. I could have called Ted and redirected the search. If Roxy came back to me before I found Ethan, I'd have her drive back to the ranch and call.

Keeping a steady pace down the road and shouting his name after every inhale, I stopped less and less frequently to listen, feeling defeated. What was my next plan? "Ethan!" I plopped my hands on my knees to catch my breath.

My ears perked before my brain registered. Was that...? "Ethan!" I shouted again, though my voice sounded like gravel in a tin cup. I picked up my feet and ran flat out, believing I'd heard a high-pitched response. I stopped again. Yelled, listened.

"Here!" Closer this time.

Encouraged, I sprinted up a hill. To the right side of the road, a lone elm grew. I'd always loved that silly tree, knowing it beat the odds. A random bird dropped a random seed in a low spot where every now and again, some moisture accumulated and perhaps, the groundwater rose close to the surface. The seed sprouted and fought to exist.

I loved this tree even more now. This is where Ethan had dragged two soggy paper sacks, empty of the fifty pounds of cattle feed and probably blown out of a rancher's pickup bed weeks before. He'd propped them in the branches and constructed the sides of his fort with tumbleweeds rammed together. While not dry, it was drier than being in the open and probably a lot warmer out of the wind and trapping his little bit of body heat.

Ethan jumped up when he saw me. "It's you!"

Not waiting to see if he wanted me to or not, I threw my arms around him and gave him a mother-bear hug. "Are you okay?"

I held him back for inspection, unwilling to let go of his

shoulders. He wore full camo coveralls and an extra jacket. An Elmer Fudd cap with earflaps down held in body heat and gloves protected his fingers. Sturdy boots completed the ensemble that kept him from freezing. Still, he had to be miserable. I know I was.

Ethan's expressive eyes showed worry. "Uncle Tony told me to stay there until an old lady came to get me, but my phone died and it got really smoky inside. I thought I could maybe walk back to town."

I put an arm around his shoulder. "I'm so sorry you had to go through this."

He acted skeptical. "I'm not in trouble?"

"No." I hugged his shivering frame close to me. "Our ride is coming along soon. We'll get you warmed up and into dry clothes before you know it."

He pointed to the tree. "Did you see my shelter? I learned about that in Boy Scouts. It really helped."

A big old lump of emotion made me swallow hard to clear my throat. "You're awesome."

He grinned and puffed up. "I think Uncle Tony will let me tell that to the sheriff and stuff. Even though I'm not supposed to say anything except act all happy to be rescued and even cry. But I'm not going to cry because, hello, I'm ten."

The sound of a vehicle approaching made us stop. I'd expected Roxy from the south but this came from the north. I didn't have to see his grille emerge from the fog fifty yards ahead to recognize the unique purr of his engine. Elvis to the rescue. Too bad he had to be driven by Dahlia.

Ethan whistled. "Su-weet."

I liked him even more. "Meet Elvis, my one true love."

Ethan turned surprised eyes to me. "That's your car?"

We waited for Dahlia to stop. She flung open Elvis's door and flew out. "Oh, thank God. You're okay."

I ushered Ethan to the passenger seat. "No thanks to you." I settled him and made my way to the driver's side. I bashed into Dahlia, who seemed rooted to the road.

She sounded nervous, a little wavery. "We can put Ethan on the console between us."

I spared her one scornful glare, my foot inside the car, hand on the door. "It's only seven or so miles to the ranch."

She looked as though I'd handed her a death sentence. "But I'm not dressed for it. I don't have a hat or boots."

"Walk fast and you'll be fine." Roxy would be along before Dahlia's first shiver, but she didn't need to know that.

I hopped in Elvis, cranked the heat, made a three-point turn in the road, and gunned it to town.

On the way back, Ethan told me the plan. Tony said they were playing a practical joke on Ethan's father. The guy hadn't paid child support in two years and hadn't even called Ethan on his last birthday. Ethan thought if he went missing, it might jolt his father into realizing how much he loved him.

Tony, you lowlife. Teaching a kid to manipulate and lie. Not to mention setting Ethan up for devastation if his father didn't respond. I wanted to stuff Dahlia and Tony in a burlap sack, tie it to a rock, and drop them in the Middle Loup. Of course, that river was shallow enough they could stand up. But it would scare the bejeezus out of them.

Before we turned from the oil strip to the highway leading to Hodgekiss, Dahlia's Barbie truck popped over a hill far behind us. Roxy flashed her lights in a not-so-subtle call for me to pull over. I kept going.

Knowing lectures never work, I had to give it a try anyway. I wasn't likely to see Ethan again, so I took the only chance I had. "It must feel awful that your father doesn't pay more attention to you. But your mother loves you. And you've got an uncle who cares." That last sentence made me cringe.

Ethan looked less than thrilled with mention of Tony. "I guess."

I spoke this most important truth slowly and clearly, hoping it would sink in enough for him to remember. "You can't force someone else to be the person they should be. The only thing you have control over is yourself and how you react."

He stared at his gloved hands in his lap.

I listened to the words. *Good advice, Katie.*

I spoke gently because guilt is a heavy club. "I know you only wanted your father to pay attention to you, but a lot of good people are out in the cold, searching through the hills, worried sick about you. That's not fair."

He brought his head up to look at me, tears pooling in those sweet eyes. "I didn't think."

I patted his camo-clad leg. "I know." I bit back the rant about how Tony should have thought and how this whole fiasco was Dahlia's fault and that Ethan was only a pawn. All of that was true. But Ethan needed to own up to his part without shifting blame.

He squeaked in a little mouse voice, "What are you gonna do?"

"When we get to the Long Branch, you're going to go up to your room and take a hot shower to warm up. I'm going to call your uncle and the searchers and tell them you're okay."

He blanched. "Don't make me talk to the people. Please. Please."

A shard of my heart broke off. "No. I'll give Tony a head start so he can get to town first, pick you up, and be on your way to Omaha before the others get back."

He lowered his head, and tears plopped onto his leg, even though he was ten. He whispered, "Thanks."

I dialed the number Ethan gave me. Not surprising, Tony

didn't seem thrilled I'd found Ethan. Tony assured me he'd talk to Ted and send everyone to town.

We pulled up in front of the Long Branch, and Ethan shot from Elvis to the outside door leading to the hotel rooms upstairs. I headed to the bar.

The Long Branch was empty and didn't do much to dispel my chill. Twyla probably prepped for the searchers in the kitchen. Louise would be gathering, cooking, directing. The box of Kate Cakes greeted me, and I grabbed one just as Roxy and Dahlia jetted inside.

Roxy started in as I made my way behind the bar. "Before everyone gets in, we need to talk about this."

My phone rang, and I held my finger up to silence her. "Hi, Ted."

Roxy waved at me, her eyes wide and frantic. I turned my back to her.

Ted sounded way more excited than Tony had. "You found him? He's at the Long Branch?" Relief whooshed through the line, and I struggled with the warring ideas of Ted the Lying, Cheating, Son-of-Boiled-Turnip and Ted the Courageous, Compassionate Sheriff.

Our conversation was brief, and my phone didn't make it to my pocket before Roxy's worried jabber commenced. "I've been thinking, and we should say that Ethan showed up here. He got lost and walked to town."

Twyla had stacked thick diner coffee mugs on the bar next to insulated pitchers of coffee in anticipation of returning searchers. I filled one.

Roxy spoke quickly. "You could say you stayed back to help with the food and man the phones. We'll help Ethan to shore up his story."

Dahlia, in all her stateliness, stood in the middle of the room, as if awaiting sentencing with dignity.

Roxy, the defending attorney, pleaded the case. "Okay. You can say you found him. That will be good for your campaign, huh? You remembered a place behind your parents' house and you went there and found him."

I poured coffee. "I won't have Ethan lie."

Roxy stomped a foot in frustration but didn't argue.

I picked up another cup. "Why wouldn't I tell the truth? That Dahlia tried to influence the election by staging this circus."

Roxy shook her head at my gesture to pour her coffee. "It wouldn't help anyone. Ted didn't know about this. You know he'd have never allowed it. It wouldn't be fair to punish him for what Dahlia did."

I held the cup to Dahlia. "Coffee?"

Her lips flattened and her nostrils flared.

Roxy picked up a cup and held it out for me to fill. "You don't want to win this way. You'd rather have a fair fight."

I filled her cup. "An honorable political campaign? That's un-American."

Roxy giggled, putting a hand to her mouth to keep from spewing her coffee. "You're so funny. I see why Ted fell in love with you."

Even Dahlia closed her eyes at Roxy's cluelessness.

The glass door banged open. Two seven-year-old cowboys barreled in, each with a rope in one hand and a sack of hamburger buns in another. Louise bounced in, hot on their trail. "Mose. Zeke. Put those buns on the table. Don't make a mess."

Dahlia drew herself up as if afraid of being damaged by the twins. Roxy whipped her face toward me, clearly pleading with me.

Louise's attention ricocheted from Dahlia, to Roxy, to me. Hands full of a two-gallon Tupperware container of potato salad, stacked with a covered cake pan, and her famous Jell-O mold, Louise broke into a grin. "Sarah called. You found him! This is so great. I brought more Kate Cakes. Everyone is going to celebrate."

She plopped the food onto a table, not noticing Dahlia and Roxy hadn't moved. "Tell me everything."

Twyla sauntered from the kitchen, unlit cigarette in her mouth. "Yeah. Tell us."

Roxy swallowed hard. Dahlia managed to look down her nose at me from halfway across the room.

Through the window behind Louise, Tony charged toward the hotel door.

I took a bite of the Kate Cake. I mumbled with a full mouth, "These are excellent."

Louise huffed in her most annoyed way. "Don't be a brat."

The twins took a turn around Dahlia, swinging their ropes and whooping in cowboy fashion. She folded her arms in supreme distaste.

Roxy reminded me of Boomer, my old boxer, and how he used to try to force me to feed him my sandwich with the power of his eyes.

I washed the cupcake down with coffee. "After I thought about it, I remembered a place a kid might be. But Ethan wasn't there. I searched a bit and found him in a shelter he'd built. Resourceful kid."

Roxy released 120 psi of air and dropped to a bar stool. Dahlia's shoulders dropped from her ears, though she kept her superior countenance.

Louise's tilted head and disapproving expression shouted how much she didn't believe me.

Tony appeared outside the window carrying two duffels. He opened the back seat of a black SUV and tossed them in. Ethan, in blue jeans and hoodie, scooted after him.

"Where is the little guy?" Louise asked.

Exhaust from the SUV puffed into the gray air. I didn't really know Ethan, but I thought I might miss him for a long time. "He was pretty worn out, so his uncle loaded him up, and they're on their way home."

The passenger door of the SUV popped open, and Ethan tumbled out. He raced to the Long Branch door, and I shot around the bar. I met him as he pushed open the glass door. He sailed right into my hug.

He gave me a short squeeze, and I whispered into his silky hair, "Be good."

Without another word, he zipped out. He jumped into the SUV, slammed the door, and they drove away.

The first bunch of searchers burst through the doors with excited shouts. Roxy met them, ready to relay all the details of my heroic rescue.

Twyla tugged my arm and squinted in Dahlia's direction. "That ain't what really happened."

I stuffed the rest of my Kate Cake into my mouth. "Close enough."

STRIPPED BARE
Kate Fox #1

In this riveting novel from award-winning author Shannon Baker, a Nebraska county sheriff's wife investigates a murder —and her husband is the prime suspect.

When Kate Fox receives a late-night phone call, her seemingly perfect life on the Nebraska prairie shatters in an instant.

Eldon, shirt-tail relative and owner of one of the largest cattle ranches in Grand County, has been killed. Kate's husband, Ted, the Grand County Sheriff, has been shot and may never walk again.

And worst of all, Ted is the prime suspect in Eldon's murder.

Desperate to clear Ted's name, Kate throws herself headlong into the hunt for the real killer.

When Kate finds herself the victim of several mysterious "accidents" she knows she's running out of time. If she doesn't find out who killed Eldon soon, she—or someone else in town— may be the next to turn up dead.

But a shocking confession throws everything into doubt, and as Kate keeps digging she unearths unfathomable secrets—the kind worth killing for.

Get your copy today at
severnriverbooks.com/series/the-kate-fox-mysteries

ABOUT THE AUTHOR

Shannon Baker is the award-winning author of *The Desert Behind Me* and the Kate Fox series, along with the Nora Abbott mysteries and the Michaela Sanchez Southwest Crime Thrillers. She is the proud recipient of the Rocky Mountain Fiction Writers 2014 and 2017-18 Writer of the Year Award.

Baker spent 20 years in the Nebraska Sandhills, where cattle outnumber people by more than 50:1. She now lives on the edge of the desert in Tucson with her crazy Weimaraner and her favorite human. A lover of the great outdoors, she can be found backpacking, traipsing to the bottom of the Grand Canyon, skiing mountains and plains, kayaking lakes, river running, hiking, cycling, and scuba diving whenever she gets a chance. Arizona sunsets notwithstanding, Baker is, and always will be a Nebraska Husker. Go Big Red.

**Sign up for Shannon Baker's reader list at
severnriverbooks.com/authors/shannon-baker**

Printed in the United States
by Baker & Taylor Publisher Services